Reading
Shakespeare
Today

JULIUS
CAESAR

Katie Griffiths

Cavendish
Square

New York

Published in 2016 by Cavendish Square Publishing, LLC
243 5th Avenue, Suite 136, New York, NY 10016

Copyright © 2016 by Cavendish Square Publishing, LLC

First Edition

CPSIA Compliance Information: Batch #CW16CSQ

All websites were available and accurate when this book was sent to press.

Cataloging-in-Publication Data

Griffiths, Katie.
Julius Caesar / by Katie Griffiths.
p. cm. — (Reading Shakespeare today)
Includes index.
ISBN 978-1-5026-1043-0 (hardcover) ISBN 978-1-5026-1044-7 (ebook)
1. Shakespeare, William, 1564-1616. Julius Caesar — Juvenile literature. I. Griffiths, Katie. II. Title.
PR2808.G75 2016
822.3'3—d23

Editorial Director: David McNamara
Editor: Andrew Coddington
Copy Editor: Rebecca Rohan
Art Director: Jeffrey Talbot
Designer: Stephanie Flecha
Senior Production Manager: Jennifer Ryder-Talbot
Production Editor: Renni Johnson
Photo Research: J8 Media

The photographs in this book are used by permission and through the courtesy of:
Photoshot/Hulton Archive/Getty Images, cover; Shutterstock, front and back covers and through out the book; Unknown, possibly John Taylor of the Painter-Stainers' Company [1] (Official gallery link) Public Domain, via Wikimedia Commons, 5; Estate of Emil Bieber/Klaus Niermann/Getty Images, 9; Screengrab of William Shakespeare Twitter page, 11; Culture Club/Getty Images, 12; Unknown, Public Domain, via Wikimedia Commons, 13; Splash News/Newscom, 15; Heinz-Peter Bader/REUTERS/Newscom, 19; By Brinkhoff-Moegenburg, professional photographers from Lüneburg. [CC BY-SA 3.0 (http://creativecommons.org/licenses/by-sa/3.0)], via Wikimedia Commons, 23; Heinz-Peter Bader/Reuters/Newscom, 28; Ray Tang/REX/Newscom, 31; Christie's Images Ltd./Superstock, 36; King Lear (engraving), English School, (19th century)/Private Collection/Look and Learn/Bridgeman Images, 39; Tony Larkin/REX/Newscom, 43; Johan Persson/ArenaPal/The Image Works, 49; Belinsky Yuri Itar-Tass Photos/Newscom, 51; Kurov Alexander Itar-Tass Photos/Newscom, 52; Greg Wood/AFP/Getty Images, 55; William Blake/Public Domain, via Wikimedia Commons, 59; ANNE-CHRISTINE POUJOULAT/AFP/Getty Images, 62; © 2014 Mya Gosling, 64; Alastair Muir/Rex Features/AP Images, 66; King Lear (engraving), Henry Courtney Selous/Private Collection/Look and Learn/Bridgeman Images, 75; Tony Larkin/REX/Newscom, 78; Stephanie Methven/WENN/Newscom, 81; By Anonymous (Galerie dramatique) Public Domain, via Wikimedia Commons, 84; Illustration for the cover of 'Finding Out, Shakespeare's World', published by Purnell and Sons Ltd., London 1964 (gouache on paper), Anne Johnstone & Janet Johnstone/Private Collection/Bridgeman Images, 89; John Michael Wright/Public Domain, via Wikimedia Commons, 90; By Jessie Chapman (Own work) [CC BY-SA 4.0 (http://creativecommons.org/licenses/by-sa/4.0)], via Wikimedia Commons, 92.

Printed in the United States of America

CONTENTS

Introduction

SHAKESPEARE AND HIS WORLD

Shakespeare often wrote plays set outside of his own time. He would often reach back into the past to address an issue or theme that was central to his contemporary Elizabethan society. One of his favorite themes was power. It appears time and again, from his historical dramas based on the English Wars of the Roses to his bloody and brutal political stories like *Macbeth*.

Shakespeare himself lived through turbulent times and experienced the shift from one dynasty to another, namely from the last Tudor monarch, Queen Elizabeth, to the first Stuart, King James I. He experienced firsthand the feelings and events that accompany a nation unsure of its fate. As Elizabeth reached her final years, England had grown comfortable and wealthy under her relatively stable rule. However, she had never married and thus had produced no heirs to succeed her. England feared that she would die before naming a successor and throw the country back into civil war. This fear of chaos and need for stability is often reflected in his work. For example, *Julius Caesar* was written in 1599, when Elizabeth was sixty-six and the whole country was filled with anxiety at the fact her reign was clearly coming to an end.

Portrait of William Shakespeare

The Globe Theatre in London

Yet, despite Shakespeare's clear fascination with history, he never let it get in the way of great drama. He was known for taking liberties with historical sources, forever prioritizing a good plot over facts. In the case of *Julius Caesar*, Shakespeare drew on ancient Roman writer Plutarch's *Lives of the Noble Greeks and Romans*. However, Shakespeare manipulated dates and times in order to keep the plot moving and the action tightly paced. For example, in the play Caesar's murder, the funeral, Antony's speech, the reading of the will, and the arrival of Octavius all happen within the space of a day. This gives us a sense of events escalating out of control and heightens the dramatic effect. In reality, these events took months and did not all take place in the Capitol. Furthermore, like any true artist, Shakespeare used his imagination where he didn't have enough information, or the information lacked interest. Writers Plutarch and Suetonius both state that Caesar had no final words, but Shakespeare endowed Caesar with last words that have become so famous that many believe them to be Caesar's actual last words: "Et tu, Brutus?"

Shakespeare's skill lay not just in his language, but in his ability to make specific moments in time seem like universal experiences. Whether a political assassination in an ancient Roman city, or two star-crossed lovers in Verona, he found common human factors to play upon. In his political or "power" plays, he shows us the best and worst of humanity, and how often power can corrupt anybody. He creates flawed characters that vary from the intensely self-aware to the completely oblivious and teaches us the importance of introspection, evaluation, and critical thinking.

Chapter One

Shakespeare and *Julius Caesar*

J*ulius Caesar* is among the most often-quoted works in the English language; the most recent edition of *Bartlett's Familiar Quotations* has seventy-four selections from *Julius Caesar* alone. So it is a measure of Shakespeare's genius that few scholars rank this memorable masterpiece among his greatest plays.

Indeed this play is usually placed rather low among Shakespeare's tragedies. It lacks several of the typical elements of his work: a single tremendous hero, a great female character, lyrical verse, rich humor, a splendid vocabulary, and overpowering emotional impact.

A.C. Bradley does not include it among the Bard's four supreme tragedies in his book *Shakespearean Tragedy* (a study of *Hamlet*, *Othello*, *King Lear*, and *Macbeth*).

The original Gaius Julius Caesar

But this is not to say that *Julius Caesar* has no distinctive excellence; on the contrary, it stands out from all drama before it.

European tragedy had traditionally been a tale of the misfortunes of a great man—typically, the fall of a king, often a tyrant who deserved his ruin. Many playwrights had followed this formula. The basic conflict was external, a cautionary tale about the vicissitudes of fate and fortune (fortune's wheel was the old symbol of man's ever-changing luck).

With *Julius Caesar*, however, Shakespeare developed a new kind of tragedy, one in which he has no rival: that of the inwardly divided hero, tormented by his conscience, revealing his internal conflict in one of Shakespeare's favorite dramatic devices, the soliloquy. This psychological conflict within the hero's soul mirrors and intensifies his outer one. Thanks in great part to the soliloquy, this poet who lived over four centuries before us gives the uncanny impression of knowing us better than we know ourselves and expressing our innermost thoughts and feelings more aptly than we could.

In Shakespearean tragedy the hero is never purely evil; there is always something about him that commands our interest, respect, and usually our sympathy. His own flaws cause his downfall; but still, we are not made to feel that this is simple justice. We feel that someone both very human and very great, someone who is like ourselves yet much larger than we are, has been destroyed. Even if he has brought his fate on himself by committing terrible crimes, we feel a sense of waste and loss. Whatever evil he may have chosen to do, something of his natural dignity continues to exist even in death. Shakespeare's real subject, we see, is human grandeur itself.

No wonder Shakespeare is still loved all over the world! Cassius is half-right when he predicts, over Caesar's bleeding corpse:

How many ages hence
Shall this our lofty scene be acted over
In states unborn and accents yet unknown!

The murder of Caesar

At the time of Caesar, England was still far from being a state, and the English language did not yet exist. When Shakespeare wrote, Europeans had only recently discovered America, and English was not yet spoken here. Cassius and his fellow assassins are of course badly mistaken to imagine that posterity will honor them for saving liberty from tyranny—indeed Caesar's death helped destroy liberty in Rome and led to an era of terrifying tyrants—but it is true that the world has never forgotten their bloody deed.

Some of the actual results of Caesar's assassination may be gathered from accounts of his successors, such as Caligula, Nero, and Domitian; see *The Twelve Caesars* by Suetonius. Literate men of Shakespeare's generation were well aware of this history and had no illusions that the

High School Caesars

PHILOSOPHY, HONOR, POLITICS—SHAKESPEARE'S *Julius Caesar* can seem to have very little relevance to being a teenager. Yet, Caesar and his contemporaries are all around us, if we would only look a little closer.

Take the 2004 comedy *Mean Girls*, starring Lindsay Lohan in the lead role of Cady. The film follows Cady as she negotiates a new school. At the suggestion of friends, she joins the popular group (known as "The Plastics") with the initial desire to gain information on the group and even out the social playing field; soon, she is caught up in a power match with the group's leader, Regina George.

It's not hard to see similarities between the two settings. Both plots revolve around jealousy, power, and backstabbing. Cady begins, similarly to the noble Brutus, wanting to help her friends but believing herself above the pettiness of high-school politics. Her friend, Janis, makes an interesting Cassius character, previously scorned by Regina and looking for revenge. The Plastics are the high school's senate, dictating the laws by which the other students can remain within the "in crowd."

Regina, whose name comes from the Latin for "queen," is the high-school Caesar, both powerful and power hungry, taking

Roman politics in American high schools

"honors" for herself, such as dating senior Aaron as a symbol of her status. Even Regina's cronies can see this comparison. Regina's sidekick Gretchen is instrumental to ending Regina's reign of terror, and we see the pair's escalating tension in Gretchen's comments as they study *Julius Caesar* in class:

"Why should Caesar get to stomp around like a giant while the rest of us try not to get smushed under his big feet? When did it become okay for one person to be the boss of everybody, huh? Because that is not what Rome was about! WE SHOULD TOTALLY JUST STAB CAESAR!"

assassination of Julius Caesar had saved Rome's liberty. Some of them saw Queen Elizabeth I as a tyrant like Caesar, but it was not easy to decide what should be done; history is always full of lessons for the present, but they are seldom simple.

Julius Caesar also reflects the old debate among philosophers and Christian theologians about whether, and under what conditions the assassination of a ruler could be justified for the common good. But Shakespeare's Brutus seems unaware that some of his fellow conspirators, such as Cassius, want to kill Caesar not for the common good, but for private revenge or to satisfy their own spite.

Brutus thinks he can save Rome from tyranny by emulating his legendary ancestor Lucius Junius Brutus, who had expelled the oppressive ruling family of the Tarquins from Rome (for a short summary of these events, see the prose prologue to *The Rape of Lucrece*); this, however, turns out to be his tragic error.

Chapter Two

The Play's the Thing

Act I, Scene 1

Overview

The people of Rome—most of them, anyway—are rejoicing.

Flavius and Marullus are Rome's two tribunes—the representatives of the common people. But today, on the day of the Feast of Lupercal, February 15, they are furious. The city's tradesmen, instead of minding their shops as required by law, are out in the streets dressed in their finest clothes to celebrate the victory of Julius Caesar over Pompey in the civil war that has seen Pompey slain. As the commoners disperse, shamed by the tribunes' scoldings, Flavius and Marullus resolve to strip away any ornaments that decorate images of Caesar.

Analysis

How is Shakespeare going to build suspense about the most famous assassination of all time? This is one of the most daunting challenges any dramatist has ever faced. Note his artistry. Immediately he establishes tension between the tribunes and the plebeians they supposedly represent. The two tribunes are still loyal to the memory of the defeated Pompey; the common people are already devoted to their new favorite, the conquering Caesar. The Bard readies our minds for a clash between partisans of the old order and the champions of the new.

Act I, Scene 2

Overview

Caesar orders his wife, Calpurnia, to let Antony touch her when he runs his race in the course of the Lupercalian festival. He says that, according to tradition, this may cure her infertility and give him a male heir.

Antony agrees to this. Just then a soothsayer (fortune-teller) steps from the crowd to warn Caesar, "Beware the Ides of March." Caesar dismisses the man as a "dreamer."

As Caesar and his followers leave, Cassius takes Brutus aside. He remarks that Brutus has seemed cool to him lately. Brutus apologizes, explaining that any coolness he has seemed to show merely reflects his own internal emotional turmoil.

Guessing at what troubles Brutus, Cassius tells him that many of the most respected men in Rome, having high regard for him, wish he could see himself as he is at this critical moment in Roman history. Brutus and Cassius

The Royal Shakespeare Company's performance of *Julius Caesar* (2012)

hear the people shout. Brutus quickly remarks, "I do fear
the people / Choose Caesar for their king."

Seizing on the word *fear*, Cassius replies that Brutus
must object to the idea. Brutus says that is true, despite
his personal love for his old friend Caesar. But if he has to
choose between honor and death, he will decide without fear.

Cassius says he has no doubt of Brutus's honor; in fact
honor is what he now wants to discuss. Here he recalls a
pair of incidents that revealed Caesar's weaknesses: once
when he himself had to save Caesar from drowning in

the Tiber, and on another occasion in Spain when the feverish Caesar, in the voice of a sick girl, begged Titinius for something to drink. Cassius marvels that the Romans can now revere this pathetic man as a god.

Again the people are heard cheering Caesar. Cassius is revolted by their adulation. Why should Caesar command more respect than anyone else—such as Brutus, for example? Cassius notes that one of Brutus's ancestors, also named Brutus, is still renowned for vanquishing a tyrant (Tarquin the Proud, the villain of Shakespeare's long poem *The Rape of Lucrece*).

Brutus understands what Cassius is driving at— Caesar's assassination—and promises to discuss it later. Meanwhile, the festival games are over, and Caesar returns with Calpurnia, Antony, and others. Caesar looks angry. He tells Antony to distrust the "lean and hungry" Cassius, who "thinks too much," rarely smiles, dislikes plays and music, and seems dangerous. When Antony tells him not to fear Cassius, Caesar insists that he fears nobody, but if he were capable of fear, Cassius is the one man he would surely avoid.

Brutus asks the sour Casca, who has watched the day's events, to describe what he has seen. Casca scornfully recounts the way Antony three times offered Caesar a crown, to the cheers of the multitude; and though Caesar refused it each time, he did so with increasing reluctance. The cynical Casca, with blunt humor, has no doubt of Caesar's hunger for power. Casca will be part of the conspiracy to kill Caesar.

After Casca leaves, Brutus once more promises Cassius that he will consider what they have indirectly discussed: the assassination of Caesar.

Left alone, Cassius reflects that the honorable but too trusting Brutus will be a great asset to the conspiracy. He is frank about his own intention to use Brutus's nobility of mind for evil purposes: "For who so firm that cannot be seduced?" Brutus, known for his strict honor and love of Caesar, will give the plot against Caesar respectability. Besides, Caesar himself, who has many enemies, loves and trusts Brutus. That night Cassius will send Brutus forged letters, seemingly written by various citizens, urging him to join the plot.

Analysis

We meet Caesar; his infertile wife, Calpurnia; his friend Antony; Cassius; and Brutus, who loves Caesar but fears his ambition. A soothsayer warns Caesar to "Beware the Ides of March" (March 15); Caesar tries to dismiss him as a "dreamer." This long scene is an excellent example of Shakespeare's skill in exposition, imparting as much information as possible while preparing us for the action to come.

Notice the huge challenge Shakespeare faces: the audience knows it is about to see a reenactment of one of the most famous historical events of all time, the murder of Julius Caesar. How is Shakespeare going to create suspense about something that everyone in the theater knows will happen? As we will see, the world's supreme dramatist rises to the occasion. (Then he will surpass it with the greatest oration ever written.)

Notice also Shakespeare's wondrous character portrayal of Caesar. Although Caesar is the play's title character, he speaks fewer than three dozen lines in this scene. We will see him only once more before the scene in which he is slain; and yet he is the most vivid and colorful figure in the story, nearly every one of his lines unforgettable. (*Julius Caesar* is barely half as long as *Hamlet*; the two plays' title roles could hardly be in stronger contrast, one almost tiny, the other one of the longest speaking parts in dramatic literature.)

Cassius manages Brutus's emotions superbly. First he says he will merely speak as his friend's "mirror," showing him only what is already within him—the love of honor. But as the scene progresses, he also appeals to Brutus's vanity and pride in his ancestors, likening Caesar to the kings whom the ancient Brutus once drove out of Rome. Brutus has none of Cassius's envy or resentment against Caesar, but Cassius knows that there are other ways by which Brutus may be "seduced." When Cassius has finished, Brutus is ready to join the assassination of Caesar.

Act I, Scene 3

Overview

Nearly a month later, on the night of March 14, Casca and the great orator Cicero, famed for wisdom and eloquence, meet during a violent storm. Terrifying omens fill the skies and streets of Rome. Casca wonders whether there is "a civil strife in heaven," or if men have somehow provoked the gods. He adds that he has seen other wondrous things. A slave's hand burst into flames without suffering pain, a lion has appeared near the Capitol, women have sworn that they saw men on fire walking the streets, and owls have shrieked at noon. It all seems quite unnatural. Cicero comments that men may misinterpret such apparent marvels:

The fall of Rome

Men may construe things after their fashion,
Clean from the purpose of the things themselves.

Cicero then asks if Caesar will come to the Capitol tomorrow. Casca replies that he plans to do so, and Cicero leaves.

As the dreadful storm rages on, Cassius arrives and recognizes Casca by his voice. He scolds Casca for being afraid and argues cleverly that the storm is a warning of Rome's condition and of the evil fate it is likely to meet soon if the wrong man comes to power. When Casca takes this to be an allusion to Caesar, Cassius says simply, "Let it be who it is," adding that the Romans no longer have their ancestors' masculine fighting spirit but instead have become "womanish" in their passive submission to tyranny.

Casca observes that the Senate will reportedly offer Caesar a crown the next day, which he will be entitled to wear in all the lands Rome has conquered, except in Italy. If that happens, Cassius replies, he will use his dagger to free himself from bondage by killing himself. Casca concurs with this sentiment. Cassius says that Caesar has one excuse for being a tyrant: by acting like sheep, the Romans have made him act like a wolf. But Cassius wonders if he has said too much: maybe Casca is willing to be a slave of Caesar and will report Cassius for expressing these seditious sentiments—in which case Cassius can still kill himself.

But again Casca agrees with Cassius. The two men shake hands; Casca has joined the conspiracy to kill Caesar.

They are joined by another conspirator, Cinna. He is glad to learn that Casca has entered the plot. Remarking on the "strange sights" seen tonight, he hopes that Brutus can be persuaded to join "our party." Cassius reassures him, instructing him to carry the forged messages for Brutus. As Cinna departs, Cassius tells Casca that all that remains is to visit Brutus at his home. From the conspirators' point of view, everything seems to be going according to plan.

Analysis

Supernatural wonders break into a play that is largely notable for their absence. Astounding omens of imminent crisis abound. Cicero is skeptical about the meaning of all these signs, but Cassius manages to take advantage of them, convincing Casca after Cicero has left that they favor the plot against Caesar. He easily brings Casca into his scheme. When they encounter Cinna, he is ready to do his part to prevent Caesar from gaining the crown.

All that remains is for the plotters to clinch the noble Brutus, the most respected man in Rome, as their figurehead.

Act II, Scene 1
Overview

We find Brutus awake in his garden, brooding over whether the assassination of Caesar is justified. So far Caesar has actually done nothing concrete to warrant shedding his blood, but power may change his nature, making him a tyrant.

Brutus's servant boy, Lucius, brings him a letter that was thrown through the window. He asks Lucius to ascertain whether the next day is the Ides of March.

Brutus reads the letter. It is the familiar message: Shall Rome be ruled by a single man? It reminds him that his ancestor Brutus drove the tyrannical Tarquins out of the city centuries earlier.

As Brutus reflects further, Lucius tells him that Cassius and others have come to see him. Brutus knows that the conspirators are ready to act and that the time has come. He can no longer put off his fateful decision.

These men, as Lucius notes, have hidden their faces. Brutus dislikes their furtiveness, which implies shame at what they are doing. He reasons that if they are saving Rome from tyranny, they should be proud of themselves. Their cause is Roman liberty. Then why should they behave as if they were guilty criminals?

The Gruppo Storico Romano reconstruct the assassination of Caesar.

They enter. After expressing regret for troubling Brutus at this early hour, Cassius introduces him to the other conspirators: Trebonius, Decius Brutus, Casca, Cinna, and Metellus Cimber. Cassius proposes that they take an oath together, but Brutus argues strongly against this idea. Why should a good Roman take an oath? His sincere promise should be enough. Brutus's argument prevails.

Cassius asks whether Cicero should be invited to join the plot. The others applaud this proposal, because

Cicero's age and gravity will counter any assumption that the plotters are merely ruled by the hot blood of angry youth. But once again Brutus objects: Cicero will never join an enterprise begun by other men. Yet again, the others change their minds and defer to Brutus.

Now Cassius raises what will prove to be the most critical point of all: Is it prudent to kill Caesar alone? He urges that Mark Antony be slain, too, for he is a dangerous enemy, a "shrewd contriver," loyal to Caesar and sure to make trouble for the assassins.

Brutus vehemently overrules Cassius. Killing Antony in addition to Caesar would be "too bloody," he argues: "Let's be sacrificers, but not butchers." Caesar's death will make Antony harmless, like the severed limb of a corpse. The plotters must seem like "purgers, not murderers." Cassius tries to object, but Brutus cuts him short. The others agree with Brutus.

The clock strikes three. Here Shakespeare commits a famous anachronism, as perfectionists love to point out: the clock did not exist in ancient Rome. But this is no blunder; the Bard would have known very well that he was taking a minor liberty for dramatic purposes. The sound of the clock tolling is a highly effective way of telling us how much time has passed and intensifying suspense. The hours of Caesar's life are ticking away.

Morning is imminent, and the fateful day has arrived. But will Caesar come to the Capitol? Cassius fears that Caesar has become too superstitious lately and, after listening to his augurers (fortune-tellers) interpret the fearful omens, will stay at home.

Decius, however, allays this worry. He knows how to manipulate Caesar with flattery, no matter what the

Brutus and his wife, Portia

augurers may say. Now everyone is ready. The conspirators
will go to Caesar's house together and escort him to the
Capitol at eight o'clock.

As the others leave, Brutus's devoted wife, Portia,
comes to him. He has been behaving strangely; she knows
something is wrong. She asks what it is. He answers evasively
that his health has been bad. She rejects this answer; she
knows him too well. Kneeling, she begs him to tell her the
truth. In order to prove her devotion to Brutus, she has
given herself a gash on the thigh.

Deeply moved, Brutus tells her not to kneel; he knows that he is unworthy of so noble a wife. But instead of telling her the truth, he promises to explain everything later. As someone knocks at the door, he tells her to leave him.

The new visitor is Caius Ligarius. Brutus tells him to come along to the house of the man to whom something must be done. He will explain on the way.

Analysis

Cassius is called Brutus's "brother"; actually, he is Brutus's brother-in-law, married to Brutus's sister—a relation Shakespeare plays down for his purposes. He turns the actual Brutus of history, whom he found in Plutarch's *Lives* and other sources, into a much purer, more abstract character. (Three ancient historians repeated the rumor that the real Brutus was Caesar's illegitimate son; there is no hint of this in the play.)

Brutus's dislike of secrecy will have disastrous results for his party. Because he is philosophical himself, he expects other men to behave like impartial philosophers. This unrealistic temperament makes him completely unfit for politics in the real world of human passions. He will meet his nemesis in Antony, who instinctively knows what Brutus can never understand.

In the matter of taking oaths, admitting Cicero to the conspiracy, and assassinating Antony along with Caesar, Cassius, against his better judgment, lets Brutus have his way. Brutus wins their clashes of wills through force of character. Nobody can stand up to him.

Cassius is concerned that Caesar will heed the warnings of the augurers and stay at home. In the past, people have used many methods to foretell the future, as we still do today.

Most of these methods can be considered superstitious, such as astrology. The ancient Roman augurers often based their predictions on examination of the internal organs of birds and beasts, as is done in this play.

Shakespeare's portrayal of Portia, Brutus's wife, is fairly faithful to the ancient sources. She was in fact the daughter of the philosopher Cato, as she says in the play. And it does seem that she tried to dissuade her husband from joining the party of Caesar's enemies.

Act II, Scene 2

Overview

Like Brutus, Caesar is awake as the storm continues to rage. Calpurnia has had nightmares and cried out in her sleep, "Help ho! They murder Caesar!" He sends orders for the augurers to make sacrifices to determine what is about to happen.

Calpurnia enters, insisting that Caesar stay at home today. He says just as firmly that he will go to the Capitol. The things that threatened him, he says, looked only on his back; they will flee his face.

But this answer fails to satisfy Calpurnia. She names several bad omens that have been witnessed lately: a lioness giving birth on a Roman street, graves opening and yielding their dead, warriors fighting in the clouds, shrieking ghosts, and more. Caesar's answer is that these are warnings to the world at large, not to him in particular. He will go forth as planned. And when she adds that portents attend the deaths of princes, not beggars, he makes his famous answer:

Cowards die many times before their deaths;
The valiant never taste of death but once.

Yet as a servant enters, Caesar immediately demands to know what the augurers are saying. He is not quite as indifferent to prophecy as he pretends.

Beware the Ides of March.

The servant informs him that the latest omen is bad: the priests have cut open an animal and found no heart in it. When Caesar dismisses this omen, too, Calpurnia begs him to stay home and let Mark Antony tell the Senate that he is ill. This time he agrees.

At this moment, Decius arrives, and Caesar, scorning false excuses, instructs him simply to tell the senators that he chooses not to appear. Decius asks for a specific reason he can offer so that he will not be laughed at. Caesar maintains that he owes nobody a public reason, but for Decius's private satisfaction, he explains that Calpurnia has had a nightmare of his statue spouting blood. The quick-witted conspirator comes up with a less-frightening explanation of this vision, and Caesar finds it satisfying.

Besides, Decius adds, the Senate plans to offer Caesar a crown today. If it gets wind of the real reason for his refusal to appear, it will joke:

> *"Break up the Senate till another time,*
> *When Caesar's wife shall meet*
> *with better dreams."*

What is more, it will seem that mighty Caesar is afraid. So Caesar resolves to go to the Senate after all. Just then, Brutus and the other conspirators arrive; so does Antony. Everyone is now ready to go.

Analysis

Much of the suspense arises from our doubt that Caesar will show up. He has to—but will he? He hesitates, as his wife tries to prevent him from going and his enemies,

Paterson Joseph as Brutus and Cyril Nri as Cassius

playing on his vanity, try to trick him. The question of whether he will die is no question at all; the suspense lies in seeing how the issue will be settled. We have to admire the cunning arguments of his foes.

This scene contains much irony and humor. Caesar wants to appear firm and decisive, but he vacillates comically as Calpurnia, the augurers, and the conspirators take turns manipulating him. The most powerful man in Rome is far from what he seems.

Act II, Scene 3

Overview

Artemidorus, a writer and public speaker who loves Caesar, reads a message he has prepared for Caesar. It names the conspirators and warns him to beware of them today. If Caesar reads it, it may save his life; if he doesn't, he will probably die.

Analysis

This brief scene underscores the danger Caesar faces and heightens the tension of his impending fate. We know he is about to die, yet there is still the tantalizing possibility that he will escape his almost certain doom.

Act II, Scene 4

Overview

Portia, with the servant Lucius, desperately wants to know how Brutus is. In agitation and confusion, she tells Lucius to run ahead to the Senate house and check on him. She chances to meet the Soothsayer, who discusses his hopes to save Caesar. She is now certain of what her husband is planning to do.

Analysis

The drama continues to heighten; Caesar's peril keeps increasing. Like Artemidorus, the Soothsayer hopes to reach Caesar in time to save him.

Our own feelings are divided. We understand Brutus's belief that Caesar is dangerous, yet we also fear for his life, though of course we know he will die.

James Mason and Deborah Kerr as Brutus and Portia (1953)

Act III, Scene 1

Overview

We are only midway through the play. In a tragedy, the title character usually dies at the end. This time he dies startlingly early, in only the third scene in which he appears. Shakespeare's first audience must have been astounded and baffled. How can a story recover from such a shock to the expectations?

Caesar, accompanied by his friends and enemies, taunts the Soothsayer: "The Ides of March are come." The man retorts: "Ay, Caesar, but not gone." Artemidorus implores Caesar to read his letter, but the quick Decius, sensing his

Performance of *Julius Caesar* at the Globe Theatre

purpose, urges Caesar to consider another man's plea first. When Artemidorus says that his letter is more urgent to Caesar, Caesar says he will put his own interest last. When Artemidorus persists, Caesar thinks he is insane, and Publius (not one of the conspirators) orders him out of the way.

Hinting that he knows about the conspiracy, a new character, Popilius Lena, raises the suspense. In the confusion of the moment, the conspirators fear they have been found out. They must strike quickly. It is now or never.

Decius, with his usual presence of mind, calls on Metellus Cimber to present his petition to Caesar. Cimber, kneeling, does so. Caesar expresses disgust at this excessively humble behavior. Brutus and Cassius kneel, too, pretending to join Cimber's plea for his banished brother. Caesar is startled by these gestures, but he insists that nothing can change his mind, for he is "constant as the Northern star." When Cinna and Decius kneel too, he tells them not to bother, for even Brutus kneels to him in vain.

Casca stabs first. All the conspirators follow, Brutus last of all. When Caesar sees Brutus stab him, he cries, *"Et tu, Brute?"* (Even you, Brutus?) and falls dead. (Many readers assume that the famous words *"Et tu, Brute?"* were the actual dying cry of the historical Caesar, but Shakespeare seems to have invented them.)

After a stunned moment, the conspirators rejoice. It is a great moment for Roman liberty, they think, which will be remembered and celebrated forever. They imagine it being reenacted in plays on the stage centuries hence, in foreign languages that do not even exist yet, with themselves honored as liberators of their country. They joyfully smear themselves and their swords in Caesar's blood. Even the gentle Brutus joins in this hideous display.

Everyone except the killers leaves the scene. Suddenly something occurs to the ever-practical Cassius: "Where is Antony?" He already senses that the assassination is only the beginning.

Antony has "fled to his house amazed." But the killers are drunk with triumph and hardly notice.

Antony's servant arrives and kneels before Brutus. He says that Antony will love Brutus and cooperate with him if only Brutus explains why Caesar deserved to die.

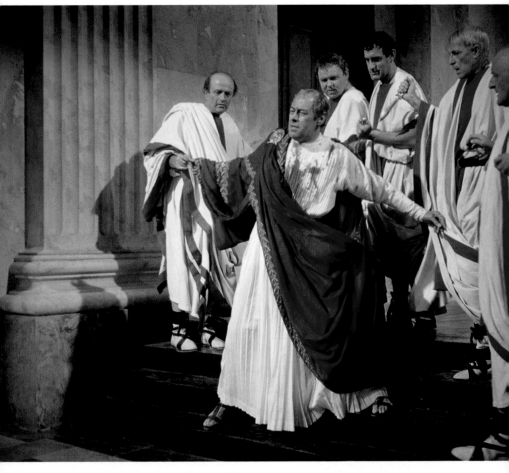

Rex Harrison as Julius Caesar (1963)

Suspecting nothing, Brutus is pleased to hear this. He remarks that Antony will prove a good friend to the conspirators. Cassius is not so sure.

Antony himself arrives. He is shocked at the sight of Caesar's body, saying, "O mighty Caesar! Dost thou lie so low?" He tells Brutus and the others that if they bear him ill will, too, they should kill him now; he will be happy to die beside Caesar.

Brutus, apologetic, tells Antony not to ask for death. Of course the assassins must seem cruel right now, but they acted out of pity for Rome and without malice toward Caesar. Besides, Cassius adds, Antony himself will share power in the new order. (Cassius assumes that power is Antony's chief motive.) Brutus pleads with him for patience until he calms the people down by explaining why Caesar had to die.

Antony shakes the bloody hands of the conspirators, beginning with Brutus. Then he resumes speaking to Caesar's corpse, with mingled grief and rage.

Cassius interrupts him to ask whether he means to be a friend to the conspirators. Antony protests that he will be their friend, provided that they give him reasons why Caesar was dangerous. Brutus agrees, and when Antony asks to speak as Caesar's friend at the funeral, he agrees again.

This is too much for Cassius. He thinks Brutus is a fool for letting Antony address the plebeians at such an occasion. What if his words inflame the people against the killers?

Brutus tells Cassius not to worry. He has an incurable habit of assuming that nothing can go wrong with his plans. He assures Cassius that he will speak first, explaining why Caesar's death was necessary, and will tell the crowd that Antony speaks by permission, giving Caesar a proper funeral. Cassius grudgingly gives in.

Brutus tells Antony that he must not speak ill of the conspirators but must praise Caesar and acknowledge that Brutus's party is allowing him to speak. Antony readily agrees to these terms.

Left alone with the body, Antony bares his real feelings. He denounces "these butchers" and predicts a ferocious civil war as Caesar's spirit demands revenge.

The servant of Caesar's nephew, Octavius Caesar, arrives and is overcome with grief when he sees the body. He and Antony weep together. Octavius, who is half as old as Antony, is still about twenty miles from Rome, and Antony tells the servant to inform him that the city is too dangerous to approach. It will be wiser for him to wait to return until Antony has tested public reaction in his speech.

Analysis

In this audacious scene, the four chief characters fully reveal themselves. Caesar, the title character, is shockingly killed midway through the story. We see his colossal ego and self-delusion exposed; he likens himself to the fixed North Star only seconds before his death.

Shakespeare takes interesting liberties with his historical sources that make Brutus's character seem more lofty and impersonal than it really was. Not only does he suppress any hint that Brutus was actually Caesar's natural son, but he eliminates Plutarch's assertion that he put a gruesome finishing touch on the slaughter by savagely stabbing Caesar in his private parts.

Brutus and Cassius achieve their purpose, in the narrow sense of killing Caesar, but of course they utterly fail to secure liberty for Rome. In fact they achieve the opposite result: they inaugurate a period of vicious civil war, which will end with the destruction of the constitutional republic they hoped to save.

Brutus assumes control of the conspiracy and blunders disastrously at every turn. Cassius's judgment is better, but he is too weak to stand up to Brutus. It is almost comical. Brutus has a perverse genius for making every bad situation worse.

The unscrupulous Antony, who cares little for Rome's traditional liberties, at least knows what he is doing and has a sure sense of how to handle men. He has none of Brutus's sentimental faith in human reason. He understands that men are ruled by their irrational passions, and that's fine by him. He never expects men to be much better than beasts.

Unlike Brutus, Cassius appreciates Antony's demagogic skill and acknowledges him as a powerful adversary. But Brutus ignores his warnings and allows Antony to take the upper hand. We are about to see the consequences of Brutus's folly.

Act III, Scene 2

Overview

The plebeians are uneasy. Their great favorite has been killed, and they demand to know why. Brutus promises them a full explanation. As he steps up to the pulpit to make his speech, another group of plebeians follows Cassius, who will also make the case for Caesar's death.

Brutus begins. His speech is short and formal, using balanced sentences. He insists that he loved Caesar, but argues that Caesar was a threat to Roman liberty. He sums up his whole argument in a single line: "Not that I loved Caesar less, but that I loved Rome more." He says he will be willing to die, too, if the good of Rome requires it. His complete sincerity is obvious.

The crowd cheers. Brutus has quickly persuaded them that Caesar was a tyrant. Their fickleness is typified by their

Paterson Joseph and Ray Fearon as Brutus and Mark Antony

irrational enthusiasm for Brutus: "Let him be Caesar!"
one member of the audience cries.

Antony arrives with Caesar's corpse, which is covered
with a bloody mantle, or cloak. Brutus, departing, tells the
people to stay and hear what Antony has to say. Some of
them grumble that he had better speak no ill of Brutus.

Antony begins, "Friends, Romans, countrymen, lend
me your ears!" He says at once that he has not come to
celebrate Caesar, but to "bury" him. This is not what
the crowd has expected to hear from Antony, Caesar's
close friend. He seems to be going further than Brutus in
depreciating the dead man. What is going on?

Antony stresses that he is speaking with the permission of Brutus and the others, all of whom are "honorable" men. Yes, Caesar was his friend, "faithful and just" to him. But Brutus says he was ambitious, and after all, Brutus is honorable. True, Caesar brought captives to Rome, greatly enriching the city with their ransoms. Maybe this showed his ambition, too? And it is true that he wept for the Roman poor. This may not have seemed ambitious of him, but Brutus accuses him of ambition, and Brutus is too honorable to lie.

Already Antony's repetition of the word *honorable* is sounding a shade sarcastic, and now Antony repeats it again, even more boldly: you all, he reminds the crowd, saw me offer Caesar the crown three times on the Feast of Lupercal, and you saw him refuse it all three times! "Was this ambition?" Now his irony is unmistakable and undisguised:

> *Yet Brutus says he was ambitious,*
> *And sure he is an honorable man.*
> *I speak not to disprove what Brutus spoke,*
> *But here I am to speak what I do know.*

He is already, only a few sentences into his speech, virtually calling Brutus a liar. He accuses the crowd of fickleness: Have they forgotten their love for Caesar so soon? Making a pun with Brutus's name, he likens the people to "brutish beasts" that have lost their reason. He pauses to let his words take effect. (He is taking advantage of their changeable emotions, not their reason.)

The plebeians begin to mutter that Caesar has been wronged. Very soon they start leaning more to Antony's version of the story. One person remarks, "There's not a nobler man in Rome than Antony."

Ray Fearon as the vengeful Mark Antony

Now Antony cuts loose, savagely roasting Brutus and Cassius, these "honorable men." There is no doubt about what he means. After only a couple of minutes, he has completely turned the tables on his enemies. The crowd is his. He holds up a parchment, which he identifies as Caesar's will. He says he will not read it, because it would have so powerful an impact on the people if they heard what Caesar has left to them.

Of course this drives the crowd wild. They insist on hearing the will immediately.

But Antony, master of manipulation, tells them to be patient, saying, "I must not read it." Being made of flesh and blood, they would erupt in fury if they knew its contents. (Antony makes multiple appeals, first to their sentimental love for Caesar and indignation at his killing, then to their curiosity and greed.)

Antony, by mentioning the will at all, professes to regret wronging "the honorable men / Whose daggers have stabbed Caesar." The crowd screams that they were traitors and villains, and demands to hear the will.

Antony comes down from the pulpit and tells the people to make a ring around Caesar's corpse, so that he may show them the man who wrote the will. He brings their passions, already violent, to an even higher pitch.

"If you have tears," he says, slightly lowering the emotional level, "prepare to shed them now." He points to the bloody cloak over the dead body, recalling the first time Caesar ever wore it, on the day of his great victory over the Nervii. (Actually, Antony was not present that day; he joined Caesar's army three years later. But neither the plebeians nor we the reader care about that; we are all swept up in the momentum of his speech.) He points out the holes made by the conspirators' stabs—Casca first, then Cassius, and finally Brutus. (Again, everyone forgets that Antony was actually absent during the assassination. Who cares?)

With his matchless sense of drama, Antony points to the bloodiest hole as the one left by Brutus—"the most unkindest cut of all," the one that broke Caesar's heart and finally killed him. (Both Antony and Shakespeare know just how to handle an audience.) This was the triumph of "bloody treason."

Antony asks the people why they weep at the mere sight of Caesar's gory clothing. Pulling the cloak off, he bids them to behold the body itself.

The effect is potent: they scream for revenge—"Let not a traitor live!"

Antony now adopts a modest tone. He asks the crowd not to let him stir them to mutiny and rage against those "honorable" men, the assassins. He professes not to be an orator like Brutus, but only "a plain blunt man / That love my friend." But if their roles were reversed, a Brutus in Antony's place would drive the city mad with the power of his eloquence. The stones of Rome themselves would come alive in fury!

As the plebeians keep calling for the conspirators' deaths—only minutes after cursing Caesar and cheering Brutus—Antony teases them for forgetting the will he spoke of. Again they call on him to read it to them.

He tells them that Caesar has left every Roman citizen seventy-five drachmas (ancient currency), as well as all his parks and gardens for them to enjoy walking in. They cheer and riot, vowing death to the "traitors."

As the plebeians riot, Antony says to himself in satisfaction:

Mischief, thou art afoot:
Take thou what course thou wilt.

A servant brings Antony word that Octavius has already come to Rome. Meanwhile, Brutus and Cassius, fleeing for their lives, have left the city.

Analysis

Brutus, seeking to calm the plebeians, thinks he can win them over with an honest appeal to their reason. If only he can prove to them that Rome's welfare required Caesar to die, he is sure that they will be satisfied. Unlike Cassius and Antony, he has no idea of the motives that really move men, such as loyalty and greed. Above all he is blind to the speed with which people's emotions can change.

Brutus's speech is a polished piece of rhetoric, in carefully balanced parallel sentences. It sounds perfectly reasonable, and the crowd applauds his argument but is only superficially moved. Their mild reception of his oration teaches him nothing. Antony is about to give him the lesson of his life in how to manage a crowd.

Brutus is sometimes compared to Hamlet, another intellectual hero who hesitates to kill, but we can hardly imagine Hamlet being so naive about human nature. Brutus really thinks he can sway the emotional mob by appealing to its better nature with fine rhetoric, as if he were addressing impartial philosophers. The street-smart Antony knows better. He realizes the obvious: that Rome is ready to explode. He sees his chance to turn the tables on Caesar's assassins and he makes the most of it.

Using bitter sarcasm and savage irony, Antony shrewdly appeals to the crowd's passions. Step by step Antony rips away Brutus's sincerest appeals as if they were bald lies. He makes the word honorable, the very word Brutus lives by, a cruel joke. He mercilessly mocks Brutus's earnest claim that he loved Caesar, making him sound utterly treacherous to his truest friend.

At the same time, Antony knows how to confuse his listeners by changing the subject. In the midst of their moral outrage at the murder, he introduces the separate topic of Caesar's will and what it provides for each of them. He uses this new subject to build suspense. In fact, he makes up the terms of the will to tickle the crowd's mercenary fancies; they are empty promises.

Truly, Antony knows every trick in the book. Through him Shakespeare displays a vast knowledge of classical rhetorical figures. Despite Antony's mastery of rhetoric, however, he always uses simple language that always seems natural, heartfelt, and spontaneous. Nobody suspects him of being anything but what he claims: "a plain blunt man / That love my friend."

It is all a horrible distortion of the reality, but the ruthless Antony has the skilled orator's art of making it seem plausible. He proves himself diabolically brilliant.

Nor is Antony, in contrast to the scrupulous Brutus, above lying and falsifying the facts for dramatic effect. He recalls the first time Caesar wore the mantle he died in, the day he defeated the Nervii. But in fact, this triumph occurred years before Antony joined Caesar's army. Another falsehood is more obvious: Antony specifies the hole that each of the killers made in the cloak. How easily we forget that Antony had left the Senate *before* the death of Caesar and could not have witnessed what he now pretends to remember in such graphic detail.

When he has finished, the conspirators have to run for their lives. Cassius's misgivings are more than fully vindicated. Why did he let Brutus overrule his misgivings?

The crowd is almost a separate character. Though fickle, they are basically prosperous and contented. One minute they are cheering Brutus; the next, they are cheering Antony and screaming for Brutus's blood.

Many have taken Shakespeare's depiction of the Roman mob as evidence that he opposed democracy. This may be true, but it might be more accurate to say that his skepticism merely reflected his view of human nature as fluid, arbitrary, and unpredictable, in both the individual and the mass.

Act III, Scene 3

Overview

Cinna, a poet, is walking alone in the street, thinking of a strange dream he had of feasting with Caesar. Something tells him he should stay at home, but he feels himself mysteriously drawn forth.

He meets a group of angry plebeians who demand to know his name and where he is going. He tries to answer reasonably, if a bit humorously, but they are in no mood for either reason or humor.

When they learn that his name is Cinna, they mistake him for Cinna the conspirator. He assures them he is Cinna the poet, but this fails to assuage them in their bloodthirsty temper. He keeps protesting that he is not Cinna the conspirator, but they kill him anyway.

Analysis

As Antony has said, mischief is afoot. He has whipped the plebeians into an insane frenzy, and a poet becomes their first victim.

As Antony has also put it, "Men have lost their reason." This is the ultimate result of his own great oration. Men have indeed turned into beasts.

Rome in turmoil

Act IV, Scene 1

Overview

Many months later, Antony, young Octavius Caesar, and Lepidus, Rome's new ruling trio (or "triumvirate"), are checking a list of names of prominent Romans, arbitrarily deciding which ones shall die (without trials, of course). Lepidus readily agrees to his own brother's death, if Antony's nephew is killed, too. Antony agrees just as quickly.

Antony sends Lepidus to Caesar's house to fetch the will. They must decide how to limit the keeping of all the promises Antony has made to the plebeians.

As soon as Lepidus is gone, Antony belittles him behind his back, saying he is "a slight unmeritable man," fit to be used only for errands, but absurdly unfit to be one of the three most powerful men in the mighty Roman Empire. Octavius asks, then, why Antony chose him to be one of the three new rulers. He can be used for the time being, Antony answers, but at this moment they must deal with the armies of Brutus and Cassius.

Analysis

The savage killing of Cinna the poet was only our first hint of the black and lawless era into which Caesar's assassination has plunged Rome. Now we see how serious the situation really is. The new rulers are freely sentencing men to death. So much for Roman liberty! Brutus's plot has brought about an even worse tyranny than he feared from Caesar.

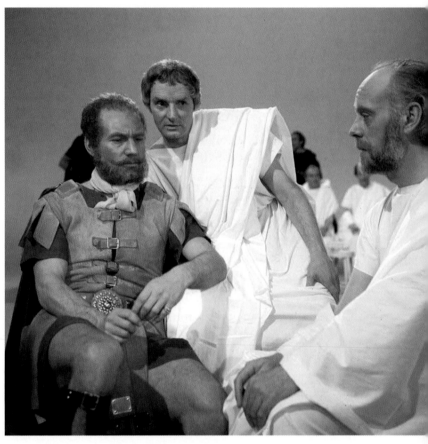
Antony and Octavius strategize.

Among other things, Antony has to deal with Caesar's will. The triumvirate cannot afford to keep the lavish promises Antony made in his speech in order to win the crowd's favor. The money he pledged—seventy-five drachmas per citizen—was part of the elaborate lie.

At least Brutus tried to tell the truth; he made no such promises to the people. He wrongly thought he was giving the people freedom, but he meant what he said in good faith. Though he was terribly naive about human nature and politics, he was at least sincere. But this is what his honesty has led to: disaster for Rome.

Act IV, Scene 2

Overview

At their camp in Asia Minor, an angry Cassius comes to visit Brutus, whom he feels has seriously wronged him. Brutus rejects this charge, saying that he does not even wrong his enemies; how, then, could he wrong his brother-in-law Cassius?

At any rate he tells Cassius to refrain from accusing him in front of their armies, who should never see discord between the two leaders. Their differences can be resolved privately, in his tent.

Analysis

For the first time we see open ill will between Brutus and Cassius. Until now their tensions have been subdued.

Cassius shows his hot temper, while Brutus displays his habitual calm. He also demonstrates a touch of typical self-righteousness when he says that he is incapable of wronging an enemy, let alone a brother.

But like the responsible leader he is, he prefers not to let others see their differences; these can be settled discreetly, out of sight.

Act IV, Scene 3

Overview

Inside Brutus's tent, Cassius vents his rage. Brutus has disgraced him by condemning one of his men, Lucius Pella, for accepting bribes and has ignored Cassius's letters pleading for him. Brutus answers that Cassius should never have tried to defend the culprit. When Cassius says that such small crimes should be overlooked at times like this, Brutus remarks that Cassius himself is widely known for taking bribes.

This really enrages Cassius, who swears that he would kill anyone but Brutus for making such a charge. Brutus's calm reply is that only Cassius could get away with such corruption. Ignoring Cassius's violent rage, Brutus reminds him that they killed Caesar for justice's sake and for "supporting robbers." (This is the first we have heard of this charge against Caesar; earlier, in Act II, the brooding Brutus was unable to think of any actual crime warranting Caesar's death.)

Cassius warns Brutus to stop baiting him. The two men exchange hot words, and Cassius all but threatens violence. Brutus refuses to be intimidated, laughing off the threat.

Cassius begins to back down, though he again threatens to do something he may regret; to which Brutus retorts that he has already done things he should regret.

There is no terror, Cassius, in your threats;
For I am armed so strong in honesty
That they pass by me as the idle wind,
Which I respect not.

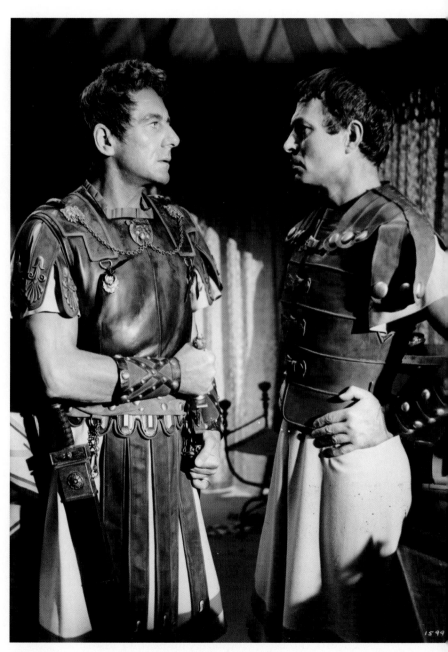

John Gielgud and James Mason as Cassius and Brutus (1953)

Yet Brutus, boasting of his own honor, now complains that Cassius has refused to give him the money he requested—the same money he accuses Cassius of raising corruptly! Nobody in this story is quite pure, not even the noble Brutus.

Cassius accuses Brutus of not loving him and pulls out his dagger, offering it to Brutus to kill him. Brutus makes fun of this melodramatic emotionalism. Cassius admits that he deserves some blame for his ill temper, and so does Brutus. In a moment they are both apologizing, warm friends again, their good humor restored.

Cassius marvels that Brutus could have been so angry. Brutus explains that he has been enduring "many griefs." Cassius urges him to bear evils like the stoic philosopher he is. Brutus reveals that Portia is dead.

Shocked by this news, Cassius marvels that Brutus refrained from killing him during their quarrel. He asks what she died of. Brutus explains that his own absence, coupled with the threat posed by the armies of Antony and Octavius, drove her to despair and suicide. Portia's suicide is foreshadowed by her earlier extreme behavior, as when she gashed her thigh to prove her "constancy." In ancient Rome, however, suicide was a matter of honor, not just depression. Both men drink wine in remembrance of this remarkable woman.

Their friends Titinius and Messala join them to discuss news of their enemies. Not only are Antony and Octavius bringing their forces to battle at Philippi, but they are also continuing their bloody purges in Rome. A hundred senators have been put to death by proscription (that is without trial); among these, shockingly, is the great orator Cicero, the most eloquent philosopher in Rome.

Messala asks Brutus whether he has had letters from Portia; Brutus says he has not. Messala tells him she is dead; Brutus seems to accept this stoically. (Scholars argue over this passage; is the repetition of the news of Portia's death a deliberate touch by Shakespeare, or a mere editing error?)

Brutus and Cassius disagree over whether to take the initiative against the enemy at Philippi. Cassius favors a passive strategy, letting the armies of Antony and Octavius wear themselves out in pursuit. Brutus thinks it is better to attack before the initiative and its advantages are lost. As usual, Cassius yields and lets Brutus decide.

As they part company for the night, Cassius regrets their earlier quarrel and expresses his deep affection for Brutus. The men retire. Brutus asks the drowsy Lucius, his servant boy, to play a few strains of music on his lute before he falls asleep. As the boy dozes off, Brutus gently takes the instrument from him to prevent its getting broken by accident.

Intending to do a little reading before he sleeps, Brutus is surprised to see someone in his tent: the ghost of Caesar. He asks who it is. It replies, "Thy evil spirit, Brutus." Why has it come here? "To tell thee thou shalt see me at Philippi," it says. Then it vanishes.

Brutus shouts, awakening all the other people in the tent. He asks them whether they have seen anything. They haven't. Caesar's ghost has appeared to Brutus alone.

Analysis

This eventful scene opens with the first open breach between Brutus and Cassius. We learn of Cassius's dishonesty, but also of Brutus's own corruption. Brutus also exposes an unpleasant moral smugness that temporarily lowers our esteem for him. But after a bruising exchange of words verging on violence, the two reconcile, and we learn that Portia has killed herself. Unknown to Cassius (and the audience), Brutus has been quietly carrying a heavy emotional burden.

This only deepens the two men's mutual love. We forgive them both for their recent faults. As the long evening draws to a close (Shakespeare makes a single busy scene seem to cover a great span of time), Brutus, alone with his servant boy Lucius, shows a movingly tender side of himself. By the time he sees Caesar's ghost we feel we have gotten to know him more intimately.

Act V, Scene 1

Overview

Antony, Octavius, and their army prepare to meet the enemy forces at Philippi in northern Greece. Octavius reminds Antony that he had predicted that the enemy would avoid the direct attack they now face. Antony replies that it is a bluff. As a messenger brings news that the enemy approaches, the two men begin to differ, as Brutus and Cassius did earlier but without anger. Not wishing to quarrel with the older Antony, Octavius asserts his authority like a monarch.

They hold a meeting with Brutus and Cassius. Sardonic and furious words are exchanged, with Antony and Octavius accusing the conspirators of cowardice, hypocrisy, and treachery for fawning on Caesar before stabbing him.

Cassius tells Brutus that these insults are the bitter reward they get for allowing Antony to live instead of killing him with Caesar. Cassius also taunts Octavius as a "schoolboy" and Antony as a playboy.

The two armies part to prepare for battle. Cassius and Brutus get ready for the worst. Cassius recalls that this is his birthday, and he has changed his mind: until now he shared the view of the philosopher Epicurus that the gods are indifferent to men's fortunes, but he has partly come to believe in divine omens.

Cassius tells Brutus that this may be their last chance to speak to one another; he asks Brutus what he intends to do. Brutus says he disdains suicide, believing that a man should endure whatever fate the gods choose.

Then, asks Cassius, you would be content to be taken back to Rome as a prisoner? Brutus refuses emphatically, but since this may indeed be their final meeting, he proposes that they make a good farewell.

Analysis

The enemies meet for the last time before their final battle. Their mutual contempt is unaltered. There is no mystery about the likely outcome. Brutus and Cassius realize that this is their last stand and that they must brace themselves for total defeat. They discuss how best to face the end. Cassius's old Epicurean disdain for the gods and their warnings has softened, while Brutus's stern philosophical disapproval of suicide also seems to be changing as he imagines being taken back to Rome as a prisoner. We are moved as we see the impact on these two strong men who imagined that they could control events.

Act V, Scene 2

Overview

Brutus orders Messala to attack Octavius's army at once. The enemy soldiers, he says, are dispirited, and a sudden offensive should defeat them.

Analysis

The excitement of the battle is conveyed by Brutus's enthusiasm. He still thinks victory is possible. As always, he is too optimistic.

Act V, Scene 3

Overview

The events of this scene are clearer in performance than on the page, where they often confuse the reader. They confuse Cassius himself, whose suicide results partly from misunderstanding.

Cassius cries out to his friend Titinius that his own men are retreating; he has killed one of these cowards himself. Titinius tells him that Brutus "gave the word too early," causing the soldiers to begin looting while they were surrounded by Antony's men. (Shakespeare is much less clear than usual here. Plutarch, his source for the details of the battle, is partly to blame. There are simply too many characters to keep track of; some of them appear here for the first time in the play. Battle scenes are always tricky to write understandably.)

Pindarus arrives and urges Cassius to retreat further; Antony's men are in Cassius's tents. Cassius, whose eyesight

The Battle of Philippi

is poor, sees tents aflame and asks Titinius, "Are those my tents where I perceive the fire?" When Titinius assures him that they are, Cassius orders him to ride and find out whether the attackers are friend or enemy. He also orders Pindarus to go up a nearby hill and report what he can see.

Cassius again mentions that this is his birthday; his life has come full circle, to end on the anniversary of its beginning. He calls out to Pindarus, who calls back that Titinius is surrounded by horsemen—that he has been captured. As Antony's men shout for joy, Cassius orders Pindarus to come back and calls himself a coward for living so long as to see his best friend captured. Pindarus returns.

Cassius orders Pindarus, a servant whom he once took as a prisoner in Parthia, to kill him. He dies on his own sword, the same one with which he stabbed Caesar. Pindarus resolves to flee this country and live somewhere else, where the Romans will never find him.

Now Titinius comes back; Messala is with him. Messala tells Titinius that Brutus's men have defeated Octavius, just as Antony's men have defeated Cassius's. Titinius remarks that this news should comfort Cassius.

The two men see Cassius's body. Titinius says this means the end of the old Rome they have known. He adds that Cassius killed himself because he thought Titinius had been captured. Messala observes that melancholy (in modern terms, depression) often causes men to make such errors.

Messala tells Titinius to find Pindarus, while he himself takes the bad news of Cassius's death to Brutus. When Messala is gone, Titinius speaks to the corpse, asking Cassius how he could have made such a mistake. He realizes that Cassius has misconstrued everything, including the soldiers' happy shouts. He takes up Cassius's sword and kills himself.

Messala returns with Brutus and young Cato. When they find Titinius's body with Cassius's, Brutus blames their deaths on Caesar's spirit: "O Julius Caesar, thou art mighty yet." He mourns Cassius as "the last of all the Romans" and promises to mourn him properly later. For now, there is a battle to finish.

Analysis

In this long and tangled scene, Shakespeare renders the chaos of war and battle. Cassius, afflicted with poor eyesight to begin with, is unable to make sense of what he sees and hears. Thinking his best friend Titinius has been captured by the enemy, he kills himself. This in turn causes Titinius to commit suicide as well. And Brutus, seeing their bodies together, concludes that the spirit of Julius Caesar has brought all this on. Of course Brutus has no way of knowing that this is just what Antony prophesied in his soliloquy only a few minutes after Caesar's death.

Act V, Scene 4

Overview

Accompanied by Messala, Lucilius, Flavius, and young Cato, Brutus urges his men to keep fighting, then he leaves with Messala and Flavius.

Young Cato boasts that he is the son of Marcus Cato. Enemy soldiers arrive, and he dies in combat. Lucilius likewise boasts that he is Brutus; enemy soldiers believe him and he is captured.

Antony comes upon them and they proudly tell him that they have caught Brutus. Of course Antony, who has been acquainted with Brutus, immediately knows better.

Lucilius assures him that the real Brutus is safe and will never let himself be taken alive. Antony explains to the soldiers that they have the wrong man, but he expresses his admiration for the brave Lucilius and orders that he be accorded the kindest treatment. He would rather have such a valiant man for a friend than an enemy.

Analysis

We see the valor of Brutus's men. Not only are they prepared to fight to the death, but they are also willing to be mistaken for Brutus. Such is the level of honor and nobility among the Romans. Antony recognizes and salutes it. As part of the dominance of action over words in this act, the audience needs to see some fighting and killing, and the death of young Cato is an additional sign on the theater stage that Brutus's army is being whittled away.

Act V, Scene 5

Overview

Brutus asks his friends and servants Clitus, Dardanus, and Volumnius to kill him. All three refuse to do so.

To Volumnius, he remarks that although the enemy has won, it is more honorable to die voluntarily than to await death at the enemy's hands. Finally, he bids the three farewell and rejoices: not only have all his friends been faithful to him, but his enemies, Antony and Octavius, have won only a "vile conquest" by usurping power. Brutus will have earned more glory in his defeat than they in their victory.

At last, with his servant Strato holding his sword, Brutus runs onto it and kills himself.

As Antony, Octavius, Messala, Lucilius, and the soldiers arrive, Strato tells them that Brutus has taken his own life, thereby denying his enemies the honor of conquering him. Lucilius thanks the dead Brutus for proving him right in saying that he would never be taken alive.

Antony gives Brutus a generous eulogy, calling him "the noblest Roman of them all." The other conspirators killed Caesar maliciously; Brutus, on the other hand, joined them because of his sincere Roman patriotism.

Octavius speaks the last words of the play, agreeing with Antony's generous assessment of their great enemy. He orders an honorable burial for Brutus.

Analysis

Caesar's spirit, "ranging for revenge" just as Antony foresaw and as Caesar's ghost predicted, has now claimed the lives of his killers. Violence has failed to save Roman liberty. The conspiracy has ended in tragedy.

In his salute to Brutus, Antony basically retracts everything he said against Brutus in his great funeral oration. There he was one of the "traitors"—who inflicted "the most unkindest cut of all." Now Antony admits that he was lying in order to inflame the plebeians. The speech was a tremendous feat of political rhetoric, but it was as dishonest as Brutus's speech was sincere.

Octavius now assumes command as Caesar's heir by giving the orders for Brutus's funeral and the sharing of the spoils of battle. Shakespeare usually gives the final speech to the highest ranking of the surviving characters. Hail, Octavius Caesar!

Analysis of
Major Characters
Julius Caesar

The play revolves around its title figure, Julius Caesar. Whether he should be regarded as the tragic hero, however, is another question. Most of Shakespeare's tragic heroes dominate the action and die at the end of the story. Caesar acts less than he is acted upon; he appears in only three scenes, two of them rather briefly; and his ghost appears even more briefly, late in the play.

Critics have never fully agreed about Shakespeare's Caesar. Is he meant to be a great leader, a vain fool, or both? We are never really told. Shakespeare nearly always leaves some room for doubt about his major characters.

Caesar was a peerless military conqueror, whose victories have shaped Europe to this day. Western civilization and the whole world are what they are because of him. In that sense, he remains one of the greatest and most important men who ever lived. It is hard to imagine what the world would be like today if he had never existed.

On the other hand, Shakespeare has no illusions about him. Caesar has a monstrous ego. He orders the Romans to write down every word he speaks; he wants to increase his power, no matter how much he gets; and he seems to want to be king, but refuses the crown when Antony offers it to him, only with obvious reluctance. Also, he often refers to himself in the third person—as "Caesar," not just "I"—and he makes huge boasts about his fearlessness and constancy, which are contradicted by his own words and conduct. While pretending to be godlike, he is wavering and superstitious, qualities that make it easy for others to

Portrait of Julius Caesar

manipulate him; and he is afraid of being laughed at. His wife's nightmares frighten him, but he tries to hide this fact from the public. Full of fears himself, he wants the world to fear him.

Shakespeare contrasts the public Caesar—mighty, arrogant, insolent, intimidating, and unique in history— with the weak and fallible private man. This difference is one of the prominent themes of the play. Unlike the conscientious Brutus, Caesar is never shown in a morally reflective soliloquy, concerned for the good of Rome. He is completely self-centered.

Still Caesar can be a shrewd judge of men, as he shows in the succinct way he sizes up Cassius, who shuns common pleasures such as plays and music, rarely smiles, reads a great deal, is a great observer of others, and "thinks too much." He has a sense of humor, which he shows by teasing Antony about his late-night reveling. He also shows a sense of humor in a negative way—in his fear of looking ridiculous if he lets Calpurnia's dreams deter him from appearing at the Senate. He is highly and intelligently conscious of appearances—a masterful politician.

It is a dramatic masterstroke of Shakespeare to have Caesar killed only halfway though the story, when the very name of the play leads the reader to expect that he will die in the final scene, like traditional tragic heroes. But the play concerns not only the individual's fate, but the rippling impact of his death on everyone around him.

The destruction of the tragic hero always affects more than the hero himself. *Julius Caesar* is unusual in studying the way Caesar's fall continues to have cascading results for friends and enemies alike.

Brutus

Brutus is often taken to be the play's real tragic hero. He imagines, in a fatal error, that he can kill the spirit of Caesar by killing Caesar's body. His great intelligence is not matched by wisdom, human insight, or any fitness for political action.

Both Antony and Cassius, sharp tacticians, run circles around Brutus. Yet they both respect the nobility of his nature, as all the Romans do. Honor is everything to Brutus. This is why Cassius knows Brutus will be a priceless asset to the conspiracy against Caesar: nobody can suspect him of acting out of selfish ambition.

Often likened to Hamlet for brooding about how he should act when faced with the supreme crisis of his life, Brutus has none of Hamlet's mercurial wit or quick, cynical perception about the people he deals with. He never makes us laugh or smile. The stoical Brutus endures the trials of fortune (and misfortune) without passion or complaint.

He kills Caesar without malice, for the good of Rome. It is an agonizing duty in which he takes no pleasure. In fact, he is so obsessed with his duty that he never faces an obvious question: So what if Caesar has actually committed no crime yet? For Brutus it is enough that Caesar may be dangerous at some time in the future. Brutus never asks whether he himself may become dangerous.

As for the actual political consequences of the assassination that all the other characters regard as vital, as far as Brutus is concerned, they hardly matter. He lacks Caesar's and Cassius's powers of observing others and judging their motives. He is completely focused on the abstract issues of right and wrong, and he is barely aware of the objective world around him. This

The noble Brutus, as played by British actor Paterson Joseph at the Chekhov Moscow Art Theatre

trait makes him universally respected, widely loved, and politically calamitous.

Brutus ignores his wife Portia's prophetic reservations. Like Caesar's wife, Calpurnia, she tries to warn and save her husband from some ill-defined peril. Brutus recognizes Portia's nobility, but he goes ahead with his fatal plan anyway. Later, her suicide will remind him that she was right, but this experience teaches him very little.

After the assassination, Brutus fails to see the danger posed by Antony, Caesar's devoted friend. He thinks he can merely appeal to Antony's reason and public spirit by arguing that Caesar was a threat to Rome and therefore had to die. Hearing this, Cassius can hardly believe his own ears. How can Brutus be such a fool? He really wants to let Antony speak at the funeral! Is he mad? But Brutus is, as always, quite sincere and earnest. His only thought is to be fair to everyone, expecting fairness in return.

Brutus is just as naive about the plebeians. He thinks it will be enough to reason with them, as if he were addressing an assembly of disinterested philosophers. Never for a moment does he suspect Antony of preparing a trap for him.

Mark Antony

If Brutus seems far more attentive to his own conscience than to the world around him, Antony is extremely alert to others and their reactions. He loves partying, drinking, sports, going to plays, and, of course, politics. Fun-loving and sociable, he has a brilliant sarcastic wit.

Antony's sense of outrage is personal, not moral; when Caesar is killed, his loyalty to his friend makes him respond violently, never mind the justifications the conspirators may offer. Nobody could be more opposite to Brutus.

Antony is also unlike Brutus in his ability to disguise his real feelings. While he pretends to accept the necessity of the assassination, he instantly resolves to use Caesar's death to incite a horrible civil war. In that way he is quite ruthless; the prospect of bloodshed does not disturb him. He is superbly masculine, and we cannot imagine him letting a woman touch his conscience as Portia touches Brutus's.

Cunningly, Antony seems to acquiesce in Brutus's act even as they stand over Caesar's corpse, but he is consumed with an inward rage that he somehow keeps hidden. We

Antony points to the bloody holes in the cloak that covered Caesar's body in a contemporary performance of the play

learn of it only when he is alone. His furious soliloquy as he addresses the body as a "bleeding piece of earth" is in complete contrast to Brutus's ethical meditations. Antony is determined to avenge Caesar's death at any cost.

Later, when he has turned the tables on Brutus and his party, Antony will lead a cynical purge of Rome's survivors, readily agreeing to the death of his own sister's son as well as well as that of the great Cicero. Moral sensitivity is not among his qualities. Yet in the end, when his enemies have been destroyed, he is capable of saluting Brutus as the noblest of all Romans, the only conspirator who sincerely tried to do what was best for his country.

Cassius

Is Cassius the villain of *Julius Caesar*, as he is sometimes said to be? The question is not easy to answer. Of course he initiates the conspiracy to kill Caesar, he enlists Brutus in the plot, he even speaks of seducing him, and his motives are more spiteful than principled.

It has been said that a story is as good as its villain, but this is a formula for melodrama; even the worst of Shakespeare's villains are recognizably human and complex enough to make some claim on our sympathies. Shakespeare himself puts it beautifully in a single line in *Troilus and Cressida*: "One touch of nature makes the whole world kin." In that sense Cassius, too, has his reasons. If he is a villain, he is at least not a monster. His mixed qualities, some of them admirable, make him akin to all of us.

One of Cassius's outstanding traits is his keen intelligence. When Antony seems willing to cooperate with Caesar's killers, Cassius is quick to smell a rat. He knows what they are dealing with: a dangerous enemy. Yet

Who's in
Control?

SURPRISINGLY, *JULIUS CAESAR* is actually one of Shakespeare's most often quoted plays. Gems such as "Cry havoc and let slip the dogs of war!" and "Friends, Romans, countrymen, lend me your ears" have been repeated, revised, and spoofed in hundreds of movies, programs, and books. One recent example is John Green's *The Fault in Our Stars*.

The title of Green's book is based on a line delivered by Cassius: "The fault, dear Brutus, is not in our stars, but in ourselves." Cassius is saying that it is not destiny that dooms humanity, but our own actions. Green's novel both explores this concept and argues against it. In *The Fault in Our Stars*, we follow two teenagers with cancer embarking on romance, while fully aware of their inevitable fate.

The concept of fate within the play is an interesting one. On one hand, the characters are fully aware of their actions, and it is their own decisions that lead them to different ends. But, as previously mentioned, omens play a huge role in the drama. The Soothsayer tries to warn Caesar about impending danger. Both the wives of Brutus and Caesar have misgivings about their husbands' plans and beg them to reconsider. Bizarre and violent omens are seen in Rome's streets. Omens are messages sent by gods as a warning to their believers. This means the gods must know the future and where all this plotting will lead. If so, then the outcome has already been

set, and there is little the characters can really do to change events. Indeed, Shakespeare himself plays with this concept by throwing circumstance after circumstance into the events that could potentially stop Caesar's murder and change the fate of Rome. Yet, we the audience know that the outcome has already been set in stone centuries before, and can only watch as things run to their inevitable conclusion.

Are we controlled by fate?

when Brutus accepts Antony's word with no guarantees, Cassius lets Brutus overrule his better judgment.

As Caesar perceived earlier, Cassius is a shrewd judge of men. He is immune to all the common amusements that others love. He has a certain self-mocking humor, but he never lets it get out of control; he is not one for belly laughs or riotous mirth. Convivial he is not. Nobody would call Cassius "one of the boys."

Caesar is also quite right when he notes that men like Cassius resent anyone they see as superior to themselves; the "envious" (that is, spiteful) Cassius hates Caesar precisely because "this man is now become a god." Cassius is forced to submit to a creature no better than himself. He must have revenge on any man who holds authority over him.

Yet Cassius really respects and loves Brutus for his nobility of nature, and he is sincerely moved when he learns of Portia's death. Brutus's rebukes for his corruption— Cassius is notorious for accepting bribes—deeply wound him, yet, after threatening to kill Brutus for insulting him, he forgives this insult as he could never forgive Caesar. There is something noble in Cassius after all.

Whatever his faults, Cassius is not amoral, and he dies with dignity on the same sword with which he killed the mighty Caesar. Shakespeare endows his character with a redeeming complexity. We may not esteem or trust him, but he is impossible to hate.

Portia

Portia is to Brutus what Horatio is to Hamlet: a touchstone. Like Horatio, she has little effect on the action of the story, but in a play dominated by men she is nevertheless an eloquent character. She helps us to take her husband's measure. We see her in only two scenes, but her death strikes a remarkable note.

As Brutus plots the assassination, he disregards Portia's intuitive reservations—she knows that something is terribly wrong, though he refuses to tell her what it is.

Portia is, as she reminds Brutus, the daughter of the philosopher Cato. This implies that she has inherited some of her father's wisdom. Cato was also an ally of Pompey and enemy of Caesar. Cato committed suicide when Caesar defeated Pompey in civil war. (In the final act of *Julius Caesar*, significantly, Cato the philosopher's son dies in battle. The war Brutus set off has wiped out the philosopher's line. Shakespeare surely intends the symbolism here.)

Chapter Three

A Closer Look

Themes

Dangers to Republican Government

Brutus fears that Caesar will restore the ancient monarchy and destroy the republic. This fear has ties with a well-known legend.

The Romans believed that almost five hundred years earlier, the self-proclaimed King Tarquin the Proud had committed many atrocities. Shakespeare had treated the evils of Tarquin's rule before, in his poem, *The Rape of Lucrece*. According to legend, led by Lucius Junius Brutus, forefather of Marcus Brutus, the people of Rome were roused to fury against the whole ruling family of the Tarquins, who were forced to leave the city.

Once Brutus's ancestor had expelled the Tarquins from Rome, monarchy was abolished. The people of Rome then established a republic, with elected officials

Cicero on the floor of the Roman Senate

representing the various segments of the population, including senators and tribunes.

This is the background against which Shakespeare's Brutus is acting when he thinks Julius Caesar is usurping power and trying to make himself a new king of Rome. He fears that representative government will be destroyed and replaced by dictatorial rule. Such tyranny, he persuades himself, must be stamped out in its earliest beginnings.

So he succumbs to the allure of violence. He cannot see any other way to preserve the Roman republic. Shakespeare shows this to be one of the flaws in Brutus's character. In any case, violence fails to save republican liberty.

The Corrupting Nature of Violence

The apparent theme of *Julius Caesar* is the battle between liberty and slavery. But at a deeper level, the play asks whether men can resort to violence without themselves becoming enslaved and finally destroyed by it.

Brutus reluctantly joins the conspiracy to kill his dear friend Caesar in the hope of keeping Romans free. He achieves the opposite result. Killing Caesar produces a chaos in which freedom and law are lost and the worst elements prevail, as when rioters murder the poet Cinna immediately after Antony's speech and, later, when Cato, the philosopher's son, dies in the general slaughter of war. Along the way we learn that even the great statesman Cicero, who has tried to stay aloof from low politics, has been marked for death in the conspirators' remorseless purge of suspected enemies. Nobody is safe.

It is all too reminiscent of the atrocities committed by modern states in the name of "security." The plot of *Julius Caesar* has lost none of its pertinence to our world. The questions it raises will always remain controversial. The world seems determined to keep generating parallel situations: assassinations, civil wars, wily propaganda, bitter clashes of public opinion, attacks on imagined public enemies, and of course an inexhaustible supply of well-meaning fools who suppose that a little more bloodletting can remedy the evils that beset us. Everyone can find their own analogies.

Motifs

The men of *Julius Caesar* are competing for glory. They are public men striking dignified poses as if they were statues (a frequent image in the play). Their speech is highly oratorical and aphoristic, fit to be chiseled on marble monuments. (There are also humble poses: Portia kneels to Brutus, Brutus to Caesar, and Antony's servant to Brutus.)

Caesar hopes and expects to enjoy eternal fame. His killers, similarly, think they will be remembered as great Roman heroes; even the self-effacing Brutus is caught up in the heady spirit of the moment, exulting that he and his fellow conspirators will always be renowned as "the men that gave their country liberty." He and Cassius both foresee their "lofty scene" celebrated in the world's theaters in the distant future.

These very public men hardly have private lives. Caesar and Brutus are the only men who seem to have wives in the play, and both ignore their wives' advice, after which the two women do not appear again. We never learn whether Antony is married. Cassius is married to Brutus's sister, but we are told nothing at all about her. The others all seem to be bachelors, for all we know about them.

This is Shakespeare's most masculine play, with only two female characters, both of whom are completely subordinate to the men. This in itself is remarkable, for in his other plays Shakespeare created an amazing range of strong, resourceful women: the sweet Juliet, the witty Beatrice, the quarrelsome Kate, the ruthless Lady Macbeth, the infinitely fascinating Cleopatra, and dozens of others, all distinct from one another. No man has ever portrayed the opposite sex with such versatility; this time it is as if he has suspended one of the most striking features of his creative genius, in order to depict the interaction of men without the distractions of sex and romance. Again and again, the men in the play profess their mutual "love."

In this testosterone-fueled work, full of reason and rhetoric, the chief characters, all calculating men, disregard the warnings of soothsayers, dreams, omens, prophecies, and women's intuitions. Caesar and Brutus both ignore their wives and take for granted that things can be settled by raw power, belittling spiritual influences. This turns out to be a grave error.

Only the cunning Antony seems not to aspire to glory. He is a peerless political improviser, and the purpose of his great speech is purely disruptive: he wants to defame Brutus and the other plotters, bringing the wrath of the plebeians on them.

Symbols

In *Julius Caesar*, blood, symbolizing death, flows freely over the stones of Rome. It is neither the hot, youthful blood of *Romeo and Juliet*, the infected and poisoned blood of *Hamlet*, nor the thick, sticky blood of *Macbeth*, but a cold, cleansing, almost impersonal fluid of monumental mortality.

As these Romans vie for fame and honor, we receive a curious impression of cold-bloodedness. Nowhere is this stronger than in Brutus's oration explaining why Caesar had to be slain. But this impression is suddenly dispelled when Antony speaks. *His* blood, at any rate, is boiling. We have already had hints of his warm nature: in contrast to both Brutus and Cassius, he loves games, sports, plays, and other common amusements, and he "revels long o' nights." He is a scrapper. He comes to fight.

Fittingly one of the dominant symbols of *Julius Caesar* is the sword, the instrument of conquest. We hear of the sword, or dagger, (and the hands that wield them) every

Blood is one of the play's strongest symbols.

few lines, until at last Brutus and Cassius stab themselves
with the very weapons they used to destroy Caesar.

Death in this play comes publicly, by stabbing and
wounds, not by age, sickness, and decay. We hear of
butchery, carving, and hewing as the fatal blades flash.
Even statues bleed. Cassius uses his dagger, Brutus his
"cursed steel," warriors in the sky drizzle blood on Rome,
and Casca points to the rising sun with his sword.

Language

We would naturally expect a Shakespearean play about ancient Rome to abound in Roman mythology, but there is almost none. The modern reader needs fewer footnotes to follow this play than any other that Shakespeare ever wrote. One passage refers to Virgil's *Aeneid* as if it were genuine history, and another makes a short reference to the "great flood" of which, according to myth, the only survivors were Deucalion and his wife, Pyrrha; there is also a mention of the legendary Colossus of Rhodes, and one of Erebus, the dark region adjoining Hades. However, Shakespeare's usual references to the *Metamorphoses* of the Roman poet Ovid, so numerous in his other plays, are entirely absent. Because the play is set in the pagan era, Shakespeare's usual biblical echoes are absent, too.

We might also expect a dense vocabulary, full of long words derived from Latin, but most of the language of *Julius Caesar* is memorably plain and pithy English, as in "He thinks too much"; "The fault, dear Brutus, is not in our stars"; "Not that I loved Caesar less, but that I loved Rome more"; "If you have tears, prepare to shed them now"; and "This was the noblest Roman of them all." Never did Shakespeare show how eloquent mere monosyllables can be. (So familiar are these phrases that an old joke has a spectator complaining after seeing a performance that *Julius Caesar* consists entirely of clichés.)

The grammar and syntax of *Julius Caesar* are also simple and clear. Shakespeare's later plays are full of language that, in both vocabulary and grammar, seems to defy us to grasp more than a fraction of its meaning on a first hearing. As a storm rages over him, to take a random example,

King Lear cries out:

Let the great gods, That keep this dreadful
pudderr o'er our heads, Find out their enemies
now. Tremble, thou wretch That hast within thee
undivulged crimes Unwhipped of justice; hide thee,
thou bloody hand, Thou perjured and thou simular
man of virtue That art incestuous; caitiff, to pieces
shake, That under covert and convenient seeming
Hast practiced on man's life; Close pent-up guilts,
rive your concealing continents And cry these
dreadful summoners grace. I am a man more
sinned against than sinning.

This is difficult to understand, even baffling, and it is meant to be.

Contrast it with Cassius's perfectly lucid explanation of why he resents Caesar's dominance:

Why, man, he doth bestride the narrow world
Like a Colossus, and we petty men
Walk under his huge legs and peep about
To find ourselves dishonorable graves.
Men at some time are masters of their fates.
The fault, dear Brutus, is not in our stars
But in ourselves, that we are underlings.

These two passages suggest the range of styles Shakespeare could command. In *Julius Caesar*, he chooses to use one that makes few difficult demands on readers and spectators.

Morally abstract words dominate the play's conversation, especially *noble, honor,* and *virtue.* We feel that the characters are incessantly paying tribute to one another and advertising their own high motives—until Antony suddenly gives the word *honorable* a lethal irony with his sardonic praise of Brutus, over and over again, as an "honorable man." (He repeats the word *honorable* nine times in his speech.) This attack is so deadly that one might almost say that the word has never fully recovered from the way Shakespeare lets Antony keep scourging Brutus with it. Among literate people, it has become hard to call someone "an honorable man" with a straight face: the listener is too apt to hear sarcasm in the phrase.

As a rule Shakespeare's plays are rich in animal imagery. Though there are relatively few of them in *Julius Caesar*, the one most often mentioned is the lion. A lion ominously appears in the streets of Rome, frightening Casca; a lioness also gives birth in the street. Cassius likens Caesar to a lion that preys on the Romans because he finds them as timid as hinds (deer). Caesar himself boasts that he is a lion:

> *Danger knows full well*
> *That Caesar is more dangerous than he.*
> *We are two lions littered in one day,*
> *And I the elder and more terrible.*

Caesar is also said to be a wolf preying on sheep.

Animals in Rome are behaving strangely. Owls, nocturnal birds of prey, shriek and hoot in the marketplace at midday. Horses neigh madly. These, like the ghosts, ghastly women, and dead men walking in the streets, are all signs of some terrible event.

Interpreting the Play

Julius Caesar deals with real people and events in history, so it can never be wholly separated from related controversies about the past—disputes both ancient and modern.

To judge by every surviving indication, *Julius Caesar* was very popular from the start. Thomas Platter, a Swiss visitor to London, wrote of having seen the play performed in September 1599. Several other references to it at about the same time confirm that it was well known. Dating Shakespeare's plays is always a tricky business, but *Julius Caesar* was certainly a success in the theater before 1600.

The play was first published in the First Folio of 1623; as far as we know, it never appeared in a separate quarto edition, but the Folio text looks very good and presents few problems for scholars and editors.

It is fascinating to contrast Shakespeare's judgment of Brutus and Cassius with that of the great Italian poet Dante Alighieri. In his immortal poem *The Divine Comedy*—an account of a tour of hell, purgatory, and heaven—Dante condemns Brutus and Cassius to the lowest place in hell, with Judas Iscariot, to be eternally devoured by Satan. For Dante the pair are, like Judas, guilty of the betrayal of a friend and benefactor. Dante regards this as the worst of all sins.

For Shakespeare the assassination of Caesar is far less odious than that, especially on Brutus's side. If Caesar was guilty of subverting the Roman republic and seeking to make himself an unconstitutional monarch, his overthrow may have been justified, or at least defensible.

Modern productions of Shakespeare's play have often been more or less sympathetic to the conspirators. In some, such as Orson Welles's famous 1937 Broadway staging, Caesar was shown as a fascist ruler like Mussolini, and Brutus (played by the young Welles, then only twenty-two years old) was shown as a muddled, well-meaning liberal.

Both the history and the play are oddly intertwined with American history. Shakespearean actor Junius Brutus Booth was named after Junius Brutus, the legendary vanquisher of the Tarquins, whom Shakespeare's Brutus (and his real-life model in Plutarch's histories) claimed as an ancestor. One of Booth's several actor sons, John Wilkes Booth, the killer of Abraham Lincoln, played Shakespeare's Brutus on the stage; Lincoln very likely saw him in the role (and in other Shakespearean roles). When Booth shot Lincoln he saw himself as a Brutus saving the American republic from a usurping Caesar. Extreme as this may now sound to us, it belongs to what was once the prevalent American interpretation of the play, which viewed Brutus as a savior of republican government against self-aggrandizing monarchists.

A curious feature of *Julius Caesar* is that Shakespeare departs from all the ancient sources of the story—Plutarch, Appian, and Suetonius. They all report that Brutus was rumored to be Caesar's bastard son, the result of a love affair between Caesar and Brutus's mother, Servilia.

This fact in itself could have furnished the premise of a fascinating play, but Shakespeare never mentions it or even hints at it. Instead he has chosen to write a *political* play, without such rich private motivations complicating its plot about public men striving for power.

Orson Welles, reviewing a script in 1938.

In his rebuttal to Brutus, Antony implies that Caesar's killers, despite the lofty reasons they claimed for the act, were driven by their "private griefs"; in his mind, politics is always personal. This is why the play still grips us. But it also raises issues especially close to the hearts of Americans, who trace the birth of their "republican form of government," as the US Constitution calls it, to their rejection of British monarchical rule in 1776.

Like so many of Shakespeare's tragedies, *Julius Caesar* shows the ultimate futility of force and violence in human affairs. The "spirit of Caesar" is more than a ghost; it is the spirit of power, conquest, and domination. Brutus succumbs to the delusion that he can defeat Caesar's spirit by Caesar's means.

Cassius and the others never question this. They assume that violence and treachery are the only ways to achieve anything in politics, whereas before his seduction, Brutus believes in appealing to men's better natures by reason and persuasion.

Brutus's oratory, though intelligent on the surface, proves uninspiring when he tries to justify the bloody methods to which he has resorted. He is essentially too good for politics, which is why, paradoxically, he is no good at politics. A man like Antony lives at the passionate level of the plebeians and instinctively understands them far better than Brutus ever can. By sharing and expressing their feelings, the "plain blunt man" controls them like a puppeteer and moves them to a fury that is indeed uncontrollable.

The Power
of Language

JULIUS CAESAR HAS, at its heart, a deep respect for and awareness of the power of language, which can literally bring down whole cities. The crowning jewel of this drama is Antony's speech to the people of Rome after Caesar's assassination. While it may seem pretty dry on the page, hearing or seeing an actor perform the speech brings alive the power and ferocity of his words. Like a true politician, Antony weaves a spell over his listeners and drives his words and feelings into the hearts and minds of his audience.

Despite its seemingly contrived set-up, the reaction the crowd has to the speech is entirely understandable. We can see a similar depth of emotion by revisiting famous speeches from throughout history.

Listen to Dr. Martin Luther King Jr.'s "I Have a Dream" speech and you can hear an epic quality in his voice as he takes the listener on a slow, burning march to the heights of rhetoric, letting his voice ring out with religious and moral fervor.

Likewise, Hillary Clinton's 1995 address to the United Nation's 4th World Conference for Women is full of rhetorical might. Notice how she collects her listeners together, addressing them both as individuals and as a wider community of international women. Follow as she walks a fine line between a calm discussion of a serious issue and a quiet anger that slowly builds to infuse the audience with a matching sense of the world's injustice.

Revisit Barack Obama's 2008 "Yes We Can" speech and see how he uses the language of community and public good, playing on a theme of unity to bring the crowd together and create a sense of teamwork and power.

Just like the citizens of Rome, we are inspired by great rhetoric.

Mark Antony creates an army using just his words.

Great speeches have always had the power to move people.

The shrewd Cassius, the "great observer" of men, knows what to expect when Antony goes to work on a mob at such an explosive moment; nobody would ever accuse him of being too good for politics!

Julius Caesar has less vivid and memorable poetic imagery than most of Shakespeare's plays. Its characters seem to prefer formal oratory and rhetoric to lyrical and metaphorical expressions of their personal feelings. They use language much more to persuade other men than to expose their own emotions, except on rare occasions such as when Brutus asks the gods to make him worthy of Portia, a moment of deep and genuine sentiment that tells us how much he must miss her after her death. He is the only character in the play who makes our hearts ache for him, yet this is not typical of *Julius Caesar*.

King Lear and *Othello* have some of the most tear-inducing scenes in all of literature; *Julius Caesar*, however, features more irony than grief. Its subject is not private sorrow, but the frustrations of men in public life.

We never see, for example, the widowed Calpurnia mourning her husband's loss. By the time of Caesar's killing, she has utterly vanished from the story, and we are never even reminded of her again. She does not really exist for her own sake; she is of interest only as a dramatic device, like the Soothsayer and Artemidorus. Her sole function, like theirs, is to try to prevent Caesar from going to the Capitol on the fatal day. Shakespeare keeps our minds fixed on the simple question: Will Caesar keep his appointment with death and destiny? Shakespeare was above all a dramatist who, whatever else he did, had to keep his audience in suspense.

None of Shakespeare's plays contain less laughter than *Julius Caesar*. One can hardly believe that this drama is the work of the same playwright who created the hilarious Falstaff and the bewitching Cleopatra. The play is also nearly devoid of music, rhyme, and other typical elements of Shakespeare's work. Even in *Othello*, an unremittingly serious tragedy, a clown and some musicians make a brief appearance, and a comical porter relieves the horror of *Macbeth*. Shakespeare seems to want each of his plays to differ from all the others in some striking respect; he is never content to repeat his successes. If he uses a formula, he uses it with some notable variation from his previous ventures to surprise our expectations.

CHRONOLOGY

1564 William Shakespeare is born on April 23 in Stratford-upon-Avon, England

1578–1582 Span of Shakespeare's "Lost Years," covering the time between leaving school and marrying Anne Hathaway of Stratford

1582 At age eighteen, Shakespeare marries Anne Hathaway, age twenty-six, on November 28

1583 Susanna Shakespeare, William and Anne's first child, is born in May, six months after the wedding

1584 Birth of twins Hamnet and Judith Shakespeare

1585–1592 Shakespeare leaves his family in Stratford to become an actor and playwright in a London theater company

1587 Public beheading of Mary Queen of Scots

1593–1594 The Bubonic (Black) Plague closes theaters in London

1594–1596 As a leading playwright, Shakespeare creates some of his most popular works, including *A Midsummer Night's Dream* and *Romeo and Juliet*

1596 Hamnet Shakespeare dies in August at age eleven, possibly of plague

1596–1597 *The Merchant of Venice* and *Henry IV, Part One* are most likely written

1599 The Globe Theatre opens

1600 *Julius Caesar* is first performed at the Globe

1600–1601 *Hamlet* is believed to have been written

1601–1602 *Twelfth Night* is probably composed

1603 Queen Elizabeth dies; Scottish king James VI succeeds her and becomes England's James I

1604 Shakespeare pens *Othello*

1605 *Macbeth* is composed

1608–1610 London's theaters are forced to close when the plague returns and kills an estimated thirty-three thousand people

1611 *The Tempest* is written

1613 The Globe Theatre is destroyed by fire

1614 The reopening of the Globe

1616 Shakespeare dies on April 23

1623 Anne Hathaway, Shakespeare's widow, dies; a collection of Shakespeare's plays, known as the First Folio, is published

A SHAKESPEARE GLOSSARY

addition A name or title, such as knight, duke, duchess, king, etc.

affect To like or love; to be attracted to.

approve To prove or confirm.

attend To pay attention.

belike Probably.

beseech To beg or request.

bondman A slave.

bootless Futile; useless; in vain.

broil A battle.

charge Expense, responsibility; to command or accuse.

common A term describing the common people, below nobility.

condition Social rank; quality.

countenance Face; appearance; favor.

cousin A relative.

curious Careful; attentive to detail.

discourse To converse; conversation.

discover To reveal or uncover.

dispatch To speed or hurry; to send; to kill.

doubt To suspect.

entreat To beg or appeal.

envy To hate or resent; hatred; resentment.

ere Before.

eyne Eyes.

fain Gladly.

fare To eat; to prosper.

favor Face, privilege.

fellow A peer or equal.

filial Of a child toward its parent.

fine An end; "in fine" means in sum.

folio A book made up of individually printed sheets, each
folded in half to make four pages. Shakespeare's folios contain
all of his known plays in addition to other works.

fond Foolish.

fool A darling.

genius A good or evil spirit.

gentle Well-bred; not common.

gentleman One whose labor was done by servants. (Note:
to call someone a *gentleman* was not a mere compliment on his
manners; it meant that he was above the common people.)

gentles People of quality.

get To beget (a child).

go to "Go on"; "come off it."

go we Let us go.

haply Perhaps.

happily By chance; fortunately.

hard by Nearby.

heavy Sad or serious.

husbandry Thrift; economy.

instant Immediate.

kind One's nature; species.

knave A villain; a poor man.

lady A woman of high social rank. (Note: *lady* was not a synonym for *woman* or *polite woman*; it was not a compliment but simply a word referring to one's actual legal status in society, like *gentleman*.)

leave Permission; "take my leave" means depart (with permission).

lief, lieve "I had as lief" means I would just as soon; I would rather.

like To please; "it likes me not" means it is disagreeable to me.

livery The uniform of a nobleman's servants; emblem.

Lord Chamberlain's Men The company of players Shakespeare joined in London; under James I they became the King's Men.

mark Notice; pay attention.

morrow Morning.

needs Necessarily.

nice Too fussy or fastidious.

owe To own.

passing Very.

peculiar Individual; exclusive.

privy Private; secret.

proper Handsome; one's very own ("his proper son").

protest To insist or declare.

quite Completely.

require Request.

several Different, various.

severally Separately.

sirrah A term used to address social inferiors.

sooth Truth.

state Condition; social rank.

still Always; persistently.

success Result(s).

surfeit Fullness.

touching Concerning; about; as for.

translate To transform.

unfold To disclose.

verse Writing that uses a regular metrical rhythm and is divided from other lines by a space.

villain A low or evil person; originally, a peasant.

voice A vote; consent; approval.

vouchsafe To confide or grant.

vulgar Common.

want To lack.

weeds Clothing.

what ho "Hello, there!"

wherefore Why.

wit Intelligence; sanity.

withal Moreover; nevertheless.

without Outside.

would Wish.

SUGGESTED ESSAY TOPICS

1. Does *Julius Caesar* have a villain? Who is most responsible for the evil in the story?

2. How might the play have been different if Brutus were identified, as in Shakespeare's historical sources, as Caesar's illegitimate son?

3. Caesar and Brutus both ignore their wives' misgivings and advice, as well as supernatural omens. How does this affect the outcome of events?

4. Before Julius Caesar, Rome was a republic, ruled by the Senate and various officers who held limited powers. After him, it was ruled by all-powerful emperors, called "Caesars." The surname had become a title; a revolution occurred. Discuss what this tells us about the conspirators' aim of saving the Roman republic from Julius Caesar's alleged monarchical ambition.

5. Do the characters of *Julius Caesar* remind you of any figures in American politics today? What do you think Shakespeare would have thought of modern democracy?

TEST YOUR MEMORY

1. At the beginning of the play, the common people are celebrating the defeat of whom?
a) Julius Caesar b) Pompey the Great
c) Lucius Junius Brutus d) Caius Ligarius

2. What has Mark Antony offered Caesar?
a) a sword b) an olive branch
c) a crown d) his daughter's hand in marriage

3. What is Caesar's wife's affliction?
a) sterility b) poverty c) ambition d) the plague

4. Caesar's wife is …
a) Cleopatra b) Portia c) Calpurnia d) Octavia

5. How are Brutus and Cassius related? They are …
a) old enemies b) cousins c) classmates d) brothers-in-law

6. Who is Cicero?
a) a gladiator b) a chariot driver
c) a tribune of the people d) an orator

7. Who is Lucius?
a) a conspirator b) Brutus's servant c) a gladiator d) an orator

8. Who is Portia's father?
a) Caesar b) Brutus c) Cato d) Metellus Cimber

9. Calpurnia dreams of …
a) an earthquake b) lions in the streets c) a murder d) civil war

10. The conspirators persuade Caesar to come to the
Capitol by …
a) threatening him b) playing on his vanity
c) enlisting Antony's help d) winning Calpurnia's support

11. To what heavenly body does Caesar liken himself?
a) the sun b) the moon c) Ursa Major d) the North Star

12. Who is the first to stab Caesar?
a) Casca b) Brutus c) Cassius d) Cimber

13. Antony promises every Roman citizen …
a) money b) glory c) freedom d) peace

14. Cinna the poet is killed by …
a) Cinna the conspirator b) a mob c) Casca d) accident

15. Julius Caesar's nephew is …
a) Lucius b) Romulus c) Remus d) Octavius

16. What happens to Cicero under the new regime?
a) he receives new honors b) he is put to death
c) his writings are publicly burned d) he is paid for his services

17. Who was Marcus Brutus's famous ancestor?
a) Titus Andronicus b) Caius Marcius Coriolanus
c) Lucius Junius Brutus d) Cominius

18. Brutus accuses Cassius of …
a) murder b) treason c) feigning illness d) taking bribes

19. Where does Caesar's ghost say he will meet Brutus?
a) at Philippi b) at Rome c) in Hades d) in Athens

20. Cassius dies on …
a) the Ides of March b) his birthday
c) the anniversary of the assassination d) a Roman holiday

Answer Key

1. b; 2. c; 3. a; 4. c; 5. d; 6. d; 7. b; 8. c; 9. c; 10. b;
11. d; 12. a; 13. a; 14. b; 15. d; 16. b; 17. c; 18. d; 19. a; 20. b

FURTHER INFORMATION

Books

Ackroyd, Peter. *Shakespeare: The Biography*. New York: Nan A. Talese, 2005.

Dunton-Downer, Leslie, and Alan Riding. *The Essential Shakespeare Handbook*. New York: Dorling-Kindersley, 2004.

Shakespeare, William. *The Oxford Shakespeare: Julius Caesar*. New York: Oxford Paperbacks, 2009.

Shakespeare, William, and Adam Sexton. *Shakespeare's Julius Caesar: The Manga Edition*. Hoboken, NJ: Wiley Publishing, 2008.

Websites

Absolute Shakespeare
www.absoluteshakespeare.com

Absolute Shakespeare is a resource for the Bard's plays, sonnets, and poems and includes summaries, quotes, films, trivia, and more.

Julius Caesar: The Play by William Shakespeare

www.william-shakespeare.info/shakespeare-play-julius-caesar.htm

This site provides the entire script of the play as well as a wealth of information related to it.

Play Shakespeare

www.playshakespeare.com

"The Ultimate Free Shakespeare Resource" features all the play texts with an online glossary, reviews, a discussion forum, and links to festivals worldwide.

Films

Julius Caesar, directed by Joseph L. Mankiewicz, 1953. Cast: Louis Calhern as Caesar, James Mason as Brutus, Marlon Brando as Antony, John Gielgud as Cassius, Greer Garson as Calpurnia, and Deborah Kerr as Portia.

Julius Caesar, directed by Stuart Burge, 1970. Cast: John Gielgud as Caesar, Charlton Heston as Mark Antony, Jason Robards as Brutus, Diana Rigg as Portia, and Robert Vaughn as Casca.

Audiobook

Julius Caesar (Arkangel Shakespeare). BBC Audiobooks America: 2005. Performed by Michael Feast, Adrian Lester, and the Arkangel cast.

Recording

Julius Caesar has been recorded many times. One of the finest recordings was directed by Howard Sackler in 1964, with an excellent cast headed by Anthony Quayle as Brutus, Ralph Richardson as Caesar, and Alan Bates as Antony.

BIBLIOGRAPHY

Bate, Jonathan, and Eric Rasmussen, eds. *William Shakespeare Complete Works (Modern Library)*. New York: Random House, 2007.

Bloom, Harold. *Shakespeare: The Invention of the Human*. New York: Riverhead Books, 1998.

Burgess, Anthony. *Shakespeare*. New York: Alfred A. Knopf, 1970.

Chute, Marchette. *Shakespeare of London*. New York: Dutton, 1949.

Garber, Marjorie. *Shakespeare After All*. New York: Pantheon, 2004.

Goddard, Harold C. *The Meaning of Shakespeare*. Chicago: University of Chicago Press, 1951.

Greenblatt, Stephen. *Will in the World: How Shakespeare Became Shakespeare*. New York: W. W. Norton & Company, 2004.

Honan, Park. *Shakespeare: A Life*. New York: Oxford University Press, 1998.

Schoenbaum, Samuel. *William Shakespeare: A Documentary Life*. New York: Oxford University Press, 1975.

————. *William Shakespeare: Records and Images*. New York: Oxford University Press, 1981.

Traversi, D. L. *An Approach to Shakespeare*. Palo Alto, CA: Stanford University Press, 1957.

Van Doren, Mark. *Shakespeare*. Garden City, NY: Doubleday, 1939.

INDEX

ABOUT THE AUTHOR

Katie Griffiths is a self-confessed bookaholic and began her love of Shakespeare at an early age. She studied English Literature at University of Edinburgh, where her addictions were further encouraged. She now lives in Hangzhou, China, where she teaches English. This is her fifth title for young people. Find her at katiegriffiths.org.